BOOK OF BEASTS

Ticktock

An Hachette UK Company
www.hachette.co.uk

First published in the USA in 2013 by Ticktock, an imprint of
Octopus Publishing Group Ltd
Endeavour House
189 Shaftesbury Avenue
London
WC2H 8JY
www.octopusbooks.co.uk
www.octopusbooksusa.com
www.ticktockbooks.com

Distributed in the US by
Hachette Book Group USA
237 Park Avenue
New York NY 10017, USA

Distributed in Canada by
Canadian Manda Group
165 Dufferin Street
Toronto, Ontario, Canada M6K 3H6

ISBN 978 1 84898 897 2

Printed and bound in China

1 3 5 7 9 10 8 6 4 2

Project Editor: Simon Breed   Design: Ian Butterworth
Battle art and spot illustrations: Lee Gibbons   Main beast figures: Colin Ashcroft
Publisher: Tim Cook   Managing Editors: Jo Bourne, Karen Rigden
Production: Peter Hunt
Additional text: Simon Breed, Jo Bourne

BOOK OF BEASTS

Illustrations by

Colin Ashcroft & Lee Gibbons

Text by Giles Sparrow

CONTENTS

CHAPTER 1

Monsters OF THE Gods

Ancient beliefs from around the world tell bone-chilling tales of weird and terrifying creatures with supernatural powers, created by the gods for fun, for fear ... or for revenge! In the jungles of South America, the ruined temples of Greece, and the swamps of Southeast Asia, they lie in wait, ready to ambush unwary travellers – so beware these demonic deities and unholy horrors!

3.5
3.0
2.5
2
1.5
1.0
0.5
0.0

MINOTAUR

- Smelling terrible
- Using a double-headed axe in a confined space
- Ambushing and slaughtering

GORGON

- Having hissy fits
- Using a killer gaze to turn men into stone
- Having an unmanageably deadly hairstyle

XOLOTL

- Fooling demons for fun
- Discharging lethal lightning without due consideration
- Giving Aztec children nightmares

Misdemeanors

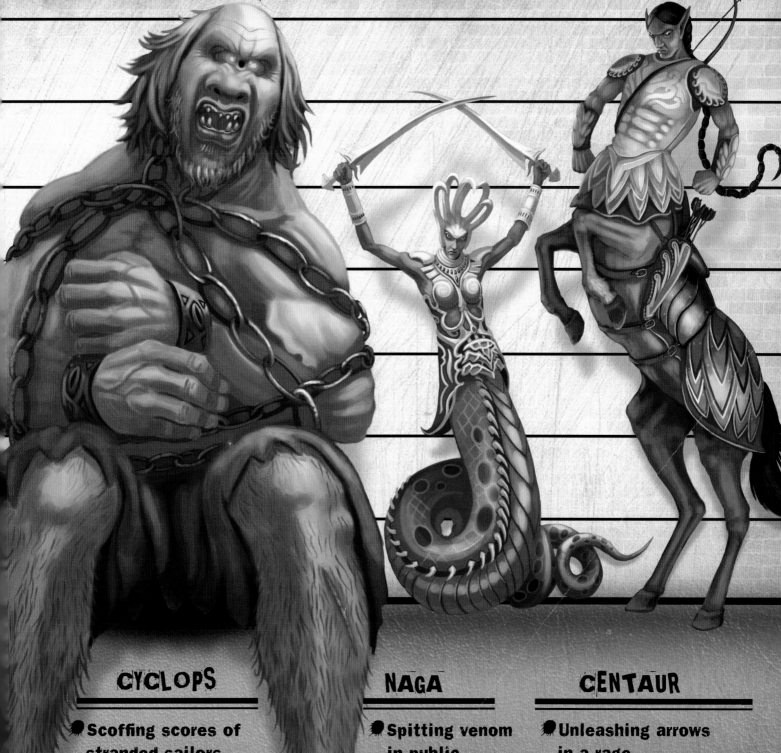

CYCLOPS

- Scoffing scores of stranded sailors
- Tearing up trees with his bare hands
- Possessing a terrible temper – and awful breath

NAGA

- Spitting venom in public
- Vicious swordplay
- Slashing swimmers

CENTAUR

- Unleashing arrows in a rage
- Being drunk in charge of four legs
- Not having a stable background

MINOTAUR

With a tremendous **stench** and a ferocious bellow, the **enormous** Minotaur emerges from the darkness of his **labyrinth**. **Imprisoned** long ago at the heart of this impossible **maze**, it once fed on human sacrifices, and still waits to ambush any modern-day traveller **foolish** enough to cross its path.

WEAPON: Doubly deadly axe

The Minotaur lays **waste** to all who enter his labyrinth, using brute force or his ferocious double-headed axe. Even the most **skilled warriors** have fallen before his might. Only brains, not brawn, can outwit him.

Monster in the maze

The Queen of Crete gave birth to the **monstrous** Minotaur after her husband, King Minos, angered the gods by refusing to **sacrifice** a sacred white bull. Horrified, the king **imprisoned** the brute at the center of an **impenetrable** maze beneath his palace at Knossos.

TIP: Unwind twine

If you don't want to get lost in the **maze**, take a ball of twine. The Greek hero Theseus unwound one to trace his path through the **labyrinth** and rescue a group of Athenians who were about to be **sacrificed**.

For the Minoans of ancient Crete, bulls were sacred. People risked their lives by performing daring acrobatics in the bullring.

BEAST RATING

- Enemies: Mortals in its maze
- Threat level 7
- Might in battle 7
- Difficulty of slaying 7
- Total 21

11

GORGON

Something hisses in the darkness, and a glint of torchlight reflects from a baleful eye. Fighting your instincts, you turn away ... just in time! To meet the gorgon face-to-face means instant stony death – as the ancient Greek heroes found out, you need to reflect carefully on your approach....

Evil eye of the gorgon

A gorgon's gaze is deadly! Make eye contact and you're instantly turned to stone. The last thing you'll see is the gorgon's evil eyes, as your body seizes up and your bones become brittle and break like chalk. You are literally petrified to death!

Serpent locks

A gorgon's hair is a squirming mass of writhing, venomous snakes – any one of which can deliver a killing bite. Some say the gorgons were once three beautiful sisters called Stheno, Euryale, and Medusa, turned into ghastly monsters by the jealous Greek goddess Athena.

SKILL: Archery

When they were still human, the gorgon sisters were **ferocious warriors**, famed for their skill with bow and arrow. Today, they still use a **bow to kill**, but they also have other, far deadlier ways of defending themselves.

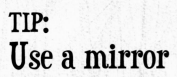

Death's head

Even after Medusa's head was **cut off**, her gaze kept its **awful power**. Perseus used it to turn a giant sea **monster** to stone. Later, Greeks and Romans used pictures of the head to protect themselves from **evil**.

TIP:
Use a mirror

That's good advice from the Greek hero Perseus. He took a highly polished **shield** with him when he set out to **confront** the gorgon Medusa. By looking only at her reflection, he avoided being turned to stone - and **lopped off her head**. If you're planning to track down her sisters, remember that everything's the other way around in a **reflection!**

BEAST RATING

- Enemies: Heroes
- Threat level — 7
- Might in battle — 6
- Difficulty of slaying — 9
- Total — 22

XOLOTL

A rumble of thunder and a **CRASH** of lightning announce that Xolotl's on his way. This Central American god has a **fearsome** reputation - he crosses the boundary between the worlds of the living and the **dead**, protecting the **souls of dead** Aztecs from **demons**, and guiding them to their resting place in the **underworld**.

Xolotl's skeletal body gives away the fact that he spends half his time in Mictlan, the Aztec realm of the dead.

Solar watchdog

While the souls of **dead** Aztecs only have to travel through the **underworld** once, the Sun has to go there every night. It's Xolotl's job to protect it on its journey, and ensure that the Sun rises again the next morning.

TRACKING: Trick prints

Xolotl can reverse his feet when he walks - a handy trick to leave misleading footsteps and shake off Aztec **demons** on his trail.

WEAPON: Fire and lightning

As if his mastery of the **underworld** wasn't enough, Xolotl is also the god of fire and **lightning**.

Xolotl's dog nose gives him a powerful ability to sniff out threats and track down lost Aztec souls when they stray from the path through the underworld. Today, nearly 500 years after most of the Aztecs were wiped out, the Mexican hairless dog known as the Xoloitzcuintle is named in his honor.

BEAST RATING

- Enemies: Demons
- Threat level   1
- Might in battle   8
- Difficulty of slaying   10
- Total   19

CYCLOPS

Still crunching the bones of his last victim, the evil-tempered cyclops lumbers from his cave in search of another meal. These one-eyed giants of Greek myth might not be smart, but they're strong, fast, and brutal hunters – find yourself stuck on an island with one, and you'll need all your wits to get away in one piece!

HABITAT: Stinky caves

A damp and smelly cave makes an ideal cyclops home – they often gather their sheep (and any prisoners they're saving for later!) inside for the night, before sealing up the entrance with a rock.

LOCATION: Islands

Cyclopes (that's the plural of cyclops!) live on small, scattered islands in the Mediterranean Sea. Wreathed in perpetual mist, the islands are not on any sea chart, because sailors who find them rarely make it back alive!

TACTIC: Aim for the eye

A cyclops's single eye is its one weak spot – although these monsters have very sharp vision, they can't judge distance very well.

If you can, steel your nerves, flatten yourself against the rock face, and try to keep still – moving will just make you easier to spot. But...

... if a cyclops does spot you, try to poke it in the eye! The Greek hero Odysseus used a sharpened stake to blind a cyclops called Polyphemus, so that he and his stranded crew could escape from an island.

Most cyclopes are shepherds and raise large flocks of sheep to eat. But raw mutton every day gets boring after a while, which may be why the tasty human flesh of a shipwrecked sailor is a cyclops's favorite treat.

WEAPON:
Basic but big
Despite being pretty dumb, the average cyclops is very strong – they often rip trees from the ground, stripping their branches to make a crude but effective club.

BEAST RATING
- **Enemies: Mortals, heroes**
- **Threat level**   6
- **Might in battle**   8
- **Difficulty of slaying**   8
- **Total**   22

SURPRISE CYCLOPS ATTACK

T wo centaurs are cantering through a treacherous valley when suddenly a massive cyclops attacks – stabbing at their flanks with a tree trunk! Quick as a flash, the centaurs let loose their lethal arrows....

NAGA

Rising from muddy waters comes the terrifying naga, her **serpent** crests rearing to spit their venom at you before her entire snakelike body **writhes** and **twists** its way onto land! Each member of this race of Asian river **monsters** is **dangerous**, unpredictable, and driven by their **voracious** appetites.

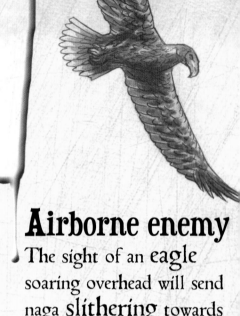

Airborne enemy

The sight of an **eagle** soaring overhead will send naga **slithering** towards the nearest river. These birds of prey are the natural predators of all **snakes**, and even naga have an instinctive **fear** of them.

WEAPON: Venom

Nagas' humanlike heads are crowned with up to seven **serpent** crests that **spit fatal poison**. They are related to the deadly king **cobras** of India and Southeast Asia. In some cases, the crests even have the heads of cobras themselves.

TRACKING: Telltale lights

Along stretches of Thailand's great Mekong River, shoreline villagers and fishermen keep a **wary eye** out for hungry naga. Glowing **fireballs** that rise from the river reveal the nagas' presence!

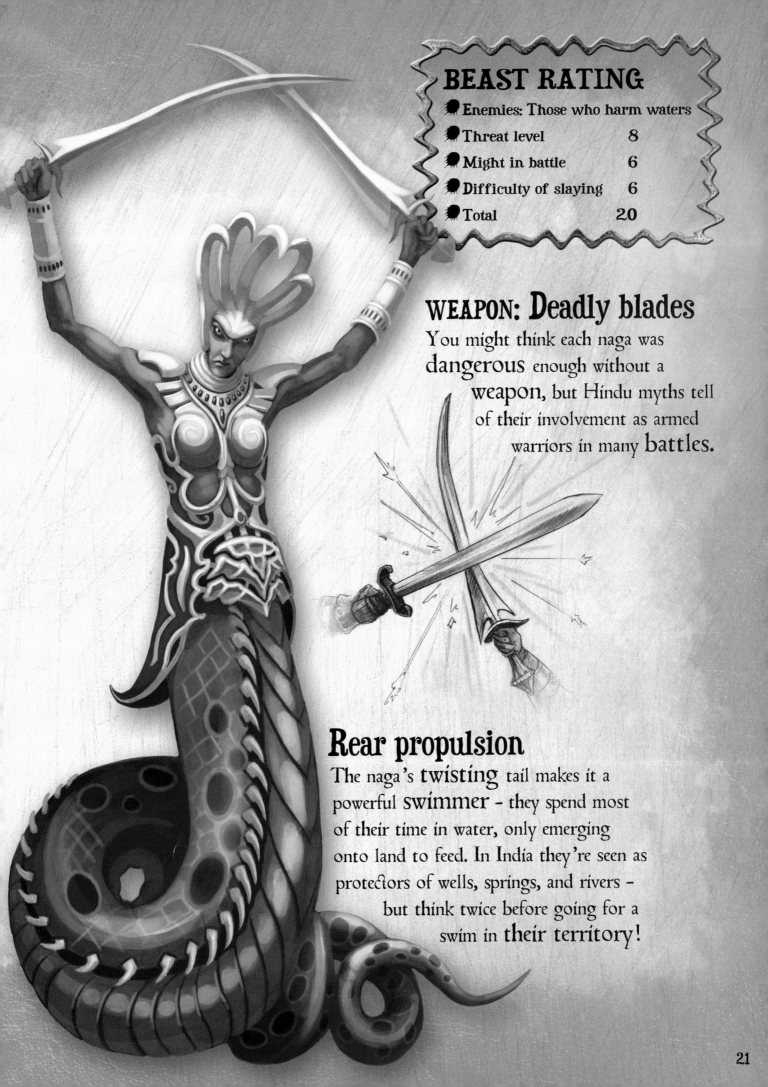

WEAPON: Deadly blades

You might think each naga was **dangerous** enough without a **weapon**, but Hindu myths tell of their involvement as armed warriors in many **battles**.

Rear propulsion

The naga's **twisting** tail makes it a powerful **swimmer** – they spend most of their time in water, only emerging onto land to feed. In India they're seen as protectors of wells, springs, and rivers – but think twice before going for a swim in **their territory!**

CENTAUR

All thundering hooves and rattling armor, the centaur pauses to sniff the air and stamp his foot, before rearing to his full impressive height. This noble but fearsome creature of Greek myth marries the body and legs of a horse to the torso, head, and arms of a man, making him a deadly opponent in battle.

Wise heads

Some centaurs have risen above their beastly nature. The most famous of all was Chiron, a wise teacher and physician, who taught many Greek heroes, including Perseus and the great warrior Achilles.

WEAKNESS: Wine

One thing that all centaurs have in common is their love of wine - they like nothing better than getting drunk and partying. So if you come across a raging centaur, your best bet may be to keep him drinking until he forgets what made him angry - or just falls asleep!

SKILL: Archery

The centaurs are famed for their archery skills - sharp eyesight and powerful arms allow them to hit their targets over huge distances. That's why the constellation of Sagittarius, the Archer, is usually shown as a centaur with a bow and arrow.

Horse-backed warriors

The ancient Greeks knew the centaurs as **vicious fighters** who descended from the steppe region between Asia and Europe to do **battle** – they were all the more **fearsome** because the Greeks hadn't mastered the art of horseback riding.

TACTIC: Trust - just!

Centaurs are smart and think with their human brains, but they sometimes let their **animal side** get the better of them – they can be rude, **untrustworthy**, skittish, and quick to **anger** – so even if you come across one that seems friendly, stay on **your guard!**

BEAST RATING

- Enemies: Mortals, other beasts
- Threat level   7
- Might in battle   7
- Difficulty of slaying   6
- Total   20

CHAPTER 2

The Undead

Every country has tales of horrific monsters that won't lie down and die – ageless, deathless, and deadly, they exist in the borderland between the living and the dead. Some are just as cunning as when they were alive, while others are mindless servants to the creators that summoned them back from the grave. Either way, it takes a lot of courage to confront these crimes against nature!

2.5

2.0

1.5

1.0

DRACULA

- Being a pain in the neck
- Stealing blood ... from the living
- Possessing lethal teeth

JIANG SHI

- High hopping without a licence
- Being in dire need of a manicure
- Scaring people witless

GOLEM

- Being a muddy nuisance
- Going on the rampage
- Mindless behavior

Misdemeanors

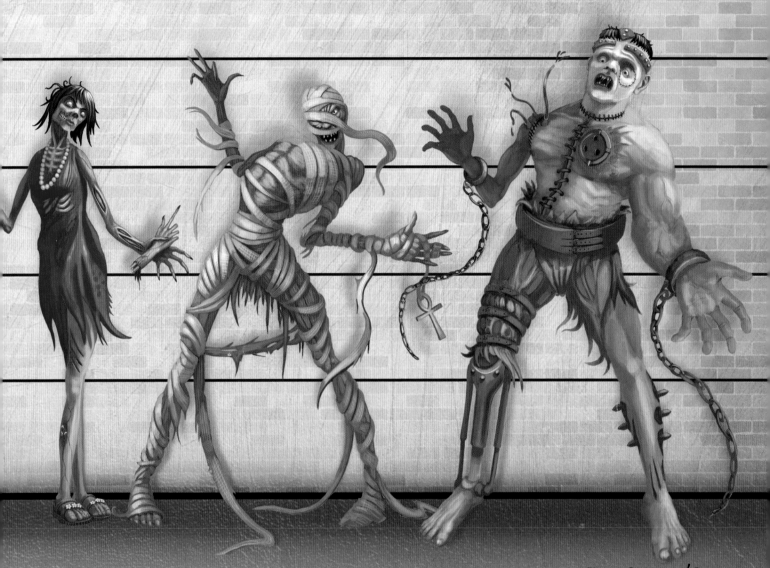

The Undead

ZOMBIE

- Generally being rotten
- Devouring the flesh of the living
- Shedding maggoty flesh in public spaces

MUMMY

- Using curse words
- Making tombs terrifying
- Staying in bed for thousands of years

FRANKENSTEIN'S MONSTER

- Murder
- Being angry with his "dad"
- Stomping after dark

DRACULA

At first glance he might seem **handsome** and charming, but you'll need to stay on your guard while **Dracula's** on the loose! Despite appearances, this **undead** nobleman is a **savage monster** with supernatural powers – and a **thirst for human blood.**

LOCATION: Transylvania

Count Dracula began his life as a Hungarian **warrior** prince, Vlad Tepes of the House of Dracul, famed for his cruel treatment of prisoners, who he **impaled** on **spikes**. No one knows how he won his immortality, but he haunts his Romanian castle to this day, lying in wait for unwary travellers.

Bloodsucker

Vampires like nothing better than **biting** into your neck and **drinking** your blood. They usually prefer to keep you alive, so they take just a little at a time. Watch out if you wake up with a pair of strange marks on your throat!

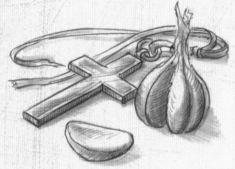

TIPS: Repellents

There are various ways of making a vampire keep its distance. Two traditional ones are: a crucifix (if you don't have one around, making a **cross** from a pair of candlesticks might work) and **garlic** – though eat too much and it might not just be vampires you're **scaring** off!

TACTIC: Check reflections

One sure way of spotting if you're sleeping over at Hotel **Dracula** is to check on your host's **reflection** – vampires don't show up in **mirrors.**

TO VANQUISH:
Strike in the day!

Vampires might be immortal, but they're not invulnerable; you can kill them by driving a wooden stake through their heart. Ambush them during the day while they're asleep in a coffin.

FIGHT OF THE FIENDS

Deep in the **secret** vaults of an undiscovered Egyptian **tomb**, Vlad Dracula soars in rage past his bloodless foe, only to be ensnared in the **mummy's bandages!**

Jiang Shi

Hopping along on one foot with its arms outstretched, this Chinese zombie might look weird, and even funny – but stand there chuckling and you'll soon see who has the last laugh! These surprisingly fast-moving living corpses will kill anything that crosses their path in order to absorb their life force.

Unfinished business

Unlike the zombies of Haiti, jiang shi seem to come back to life on their own – often when a coffin is left unburied after the funeral or struck by lightning, or when a black cat leaps across the corpse. Their restless spirits are often driven by the need to settle unfinished business.

Telltale style and skin

Jiang shi wear old-fashioned Chinese clothing – they originated in the Qing Dynasty more than 100 years ago, and don't seem to have changed their fashions with the times. Apart from their traditional outfits, the other big clue to a jiang shi's spooky nature is the ghastly greenish color of its decaying skin.

TO VANQUISH: Use seeds!

There are lots of ways to scare off jiang shi – in addition to roosters, they're scared of their own reflections, items made of peach wood, sticky rice, and bells. If you need to finish one off, however, the recommended way is to hammer seven seeds from the jujube fruit into the acupuncture points on its back – ouch!

A jiang shi's body is still as stiff as a board - which is why they hop on one foot with their arms sticking out to keep them balanced.

Night owls

Jiang shi roam the land at night, but fear sunlight and flee to dark caves and other hiding places at dawn. If you're venturing into jiang shi country, take a rooster with you - jiang shi aren't that bright, and they'll often hop off when they hear a rooster crow, even if it's the middle of the night!

BEAST RATING

- Enemies: Mortals
- Threat level   7
- Might in battle   7
- Difficulty of slaying   2
- Total   16

GOLEM

A roughly finished mass of **crumbling** clay, the golem is a shambling, foot-dragging **giant** straight out of your worst **nightmares**. Created to protect, its **violent** nature soon got out of control, before it **disappeared** into the **mists** of **history**.

TO DESTROY:
Go for the head

A glowing jewel in the golem's forehead acts as its **soul** – yank it out and you'll **destroy** the monster for good.

Out of the soil

There have been many golems. The last and most famous was supposed to have been created out of soil and mud by Rabbi Loew in Prague. Like all golem, this one was a **mindless** servant, **brought to life** to protect the Jews of the city from being **attacked**.

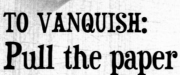

TO VANQUISH:
Pull the paper

Rabbi Loew brought the golem to life by **stuffing** a piece of paper inscribed with **magic words** into its mouth. Pull the paper out and it turns back to a lump of **clay** – but you'll have to get very close to **reach** it!

Missing – presumed ...?

The golem was supposed to be locked away in the **attic** of the Prague Synagogue, but there's nothing in there today. Perhaps the monster was brought back to **life** and is still **wandering** the world ... ?

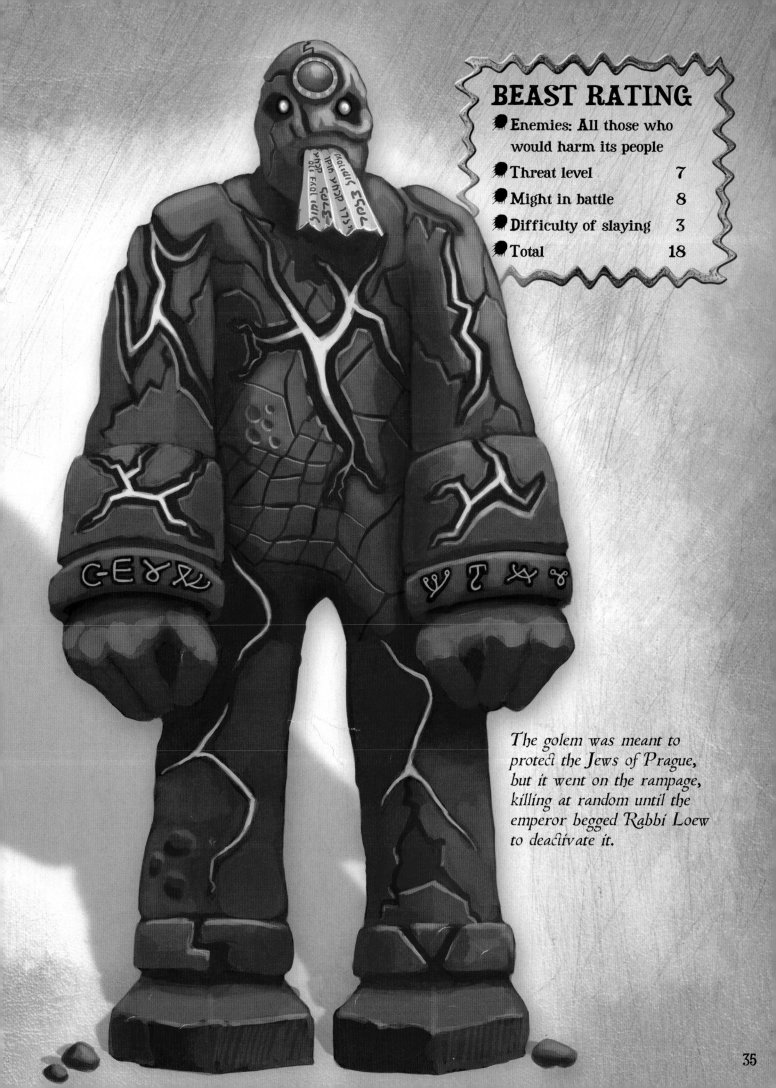

BEAST RATING

- Enemies: All those who would harm its people
- Threat level   7
- Might in battle   8
- Difficulty of slaying   3
- Total   18

The golem was meant to protect the Jews of Prague, but it went on the rampage, killing at random until the emperor begged Rabbi Loew to deactivate it.

ZOMBIE

The living dead come in all shapes and sizes, but zombies come from the Caribbean island of Haiti, where their shambling, decaying corpses are conjured back into action to do the will of voodoo sorcerers. Tireless and impervious to pain, zombies might not be fast, but they never give up - so be careful not to get a **zombie** on your trail!

TIP: Shatter the bottle

Voodoo priests called "bokors" conjure zombies from death using magic spells to trap part of the soul called the "zombie astral." Once the bokor has trapped the astral in a bottle, the zombie's body has no will of its own – smash the bottle and the control is broken.

Voodoo dolls

Sorcerors make zombies out of both living and dead people using magic voodoo dolls. When a snip of hair or something else belonging to the victim is attached to one of these crude dolls, they're transformed into a puppet with no choice but to obey the bokor's will.

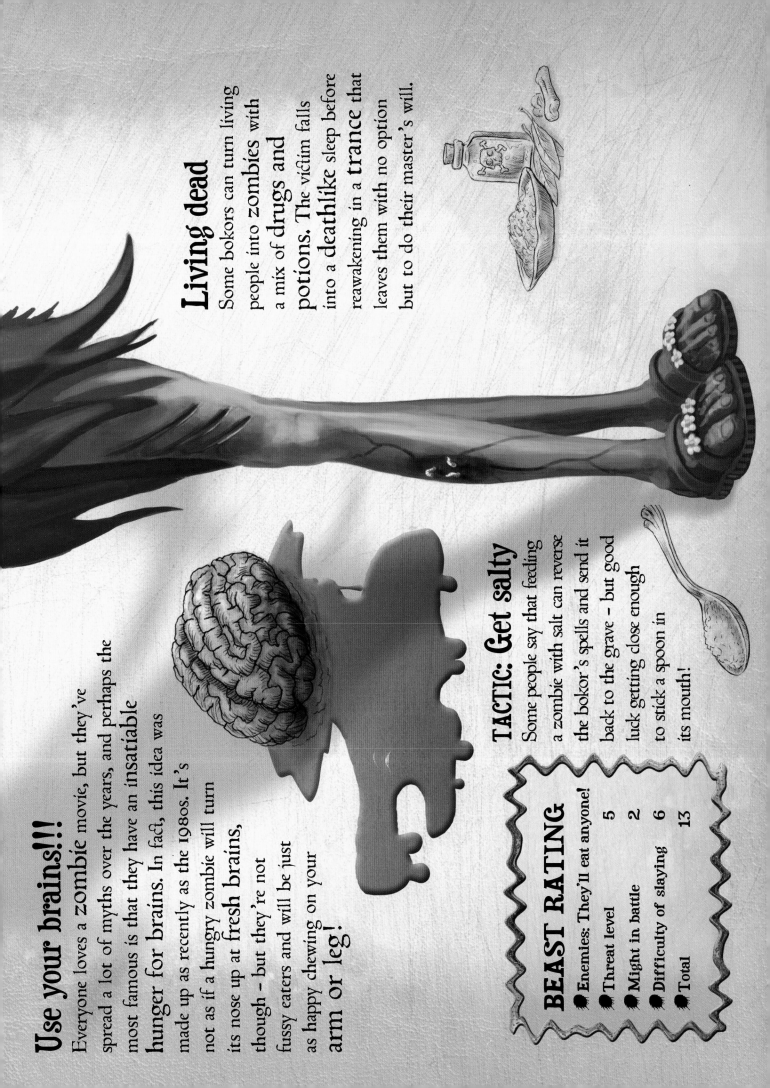

Use your brains!!!

Everyone loves a zombie movie, but they've spread a lot of myths over the years, and perhaps the most famous is that they have an insatiable **hunger for brains.** In fact, this idea was made up as recently as the 1980s. It's not as if a hungry zombie will turn its nose up at **fresh brains,** though – but they're not fussy eaters and will be just as happy chewing on your **arm or leg!**

Living dead

Some bokors can turn living people into **zombies** with a mix of **drugs and potions.** The victim falls into a **deathlike** sleep before reawakening in a **trance** that leaves them with no option but to do their master's will.

TACTIC: Get salty

Some people say that feeding a zombie with salt can reverse the bokor's spells and send it back to the grave – but good luck getting close enough to stick a spoon in its mouth!

BEAST RATING

- ● **Enemies:** They'll eat anyone!
- ● Threat level   5
- ● Might in battle   2
- ● Difficulty of slaying   6
- ● Total   13

MUMMY

Accidentally **reanimated** by curious explorers or greedy treasure hunters, the **mummy** emerges from its tomb to wreak revenge. Tattered **bandages** hold his parched and **ancient body** together, but despite appearances, he's immensely strong, relentlessly hunting down anyone who dares disturb his **eternal sleep.**

Beware of the dog

Statues and paintings of the jackal god Anubis, guardian of the Egyptian underworld, guard the mummy's **tomb**, often carrying a curse that threatens **grisly death** to all those who **dare enter....**

Pyramid scheme

Mummies are the preserved **bodies** of Ancient Egyptian kings called "pharaohs." Early kings built the famous pyramids as their last resting places, but later ones hid their **tombs** away in the desert sands.

Mummy bindings

Egyptian priests wrapped the body of a dead **pharaoh** in special bandages to preserve the body on its journey to the underworld – they couldn't have known that the same magic would bring him back to life!

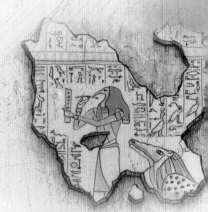

TACTIC: Coffin confrontation

The mummy rests in a huge box called a sarcophagus (it literally means "flesh-eater" – yuck!) covered in magical inscriptions. If you're going to confront him, this is the best place to do it.

BEAST RATING

- Enemies: Mortals, vampires
- Threat level   7
- Might in battle   7
- Difficulty of slaying   7
- Total   21

WEAKNESS: Body parts

The first thing a resurrected mummy will do is to try to pull himself together, tracking down the special "canopic jars" where the priests put his brain, heart, and other organs. He only gains his full strength when he's whole.

THE EGYPTIAN BOOK OF THE DEAD is written on tomb walls and on sarcophagi. If a mummy's on the rampage, it's got all the spells you need to put him back in his box!

FRANKENSTEIN'S MONSTER

Lurching out of the darkness, **electrical** sparks crackling around his fingers, comes a **horrific creature** of immense strength and cunning. Created by the obsessive, brilliant medical student Victor Frankenstein, the nameless **monster** is a **horrific mishmash** of reanimated **body parts**.

TIP: Use flames!

The monster hates fire. When locals saw the **creature**, they drove him away with flaming torches blaming him for killing the old man. Now, the **monster** roams the world in a never-ending search for his creator.

Spare parts

An arm here, a foot there ... Frankenstein stitched his monster together using body parts, stolen from **corpses** in the mortuary or dug out of the ground by **grave robbers**.

It's alive!

Dr. Frankenstein used the electricity from a **bolt of lightning** to bring the monster to life, transforming it from a patchwork **cadaver** to a living, thinking being. Horrified by what he had done, the doctor fled from his own creation.

Friendship is blind

Abandoned in the **wilderness**, the **creature** found protection with an old blind man who could not see its **horrendous** appearance. The monster taught himself to read and think, but when the old man died, the monster grew angry with his creator.

TACTIC: Short-circuit!

Electrodes on the creature's skull were used to spark its brain into life. Short-circuit them and you may confuse the poor brute long enough to escape without having to fight it.

BEAST RATING

- Enemies: Humanity
- Threat level   5
- Might in battle   8
- Difficulty of slaying   8
- Total   21

CHAPTER 3

Dragons

With a **thunderous** beating of wings and blasts of **searing flame**, the dragons announce their arrival! Magnificent, **cunning,** and vicious, dragons are the mightiest and most dangerous of all **fantastical** beasts, combining an awesome physical threat with magical powers. Some are hungry for **treasure,** but others are just ... **hungry!**

Crimes and

6.0

5.0

4.0

3.0

2.0

1.0

LJUBLJANA DRAGON

- Breathing fire within city limits
- Theft of shiny things
- Being overly defensive

CHINESE DRAGON

- Unleashing fire and lightning for fun
- Flying without wings or a licence
- Becoming invisible at will

Misdemeanors

Dragons

LAMBTON WORM

- Being revoltingly wormlike and evil
- Scoffing sheep
- Fighting knights

JERSEY DEVIL

- Scaring travellers to death
- Vandalizing public transport
- Wasting police time by flying away

WYVERN

- Breathing utterly stinky gas
- Spewing foul flames in public
- Posing as a gargoyle

LJUBLJANA DRAGON

Pawing at the ground with **vicious** claws, a ferocious dragon stands watch over the Slovenian city of Ljubljana (say *lyoo-blee-yana*). **Huge wings** beat the air and **smoke** puffs from his nostrils as he looks out for any distant threats to the city built on his **ancient** homeland.

Swamp monster

Folktales tell how the Greek hero Jason stopped off in Slovenia with his ship, the *Argo*, on his way back from stealing the famous Golden Fleece. He fought and **killed** a terrible marsh **dragon** living in a lake on the site of the present-day city.

TIP: Don't take treasure

The Ljubljana monster is a typical European dragon – **gigantic**, fire-breathing, four-legged, with a scaly hide and **vicious teeth**. Like all of his kind, he has a lust for **gold**, jewels, and anything shiny – so best to leave your small change at home!

A powerful friend

Today, the people of Ljubljana see the dragon's descendant as their protector – **statues** of him guard the bridge over the Ljubljanica River, and he appears above the **castle** on the city's coat of arms. Don't mess with this city – it's got a **fire-breather** on its side!

46

BEAST RATING

- Enemies: Those who would attack its city
- Threat level   6
- Might in battle   9
- Difficulty of slaying   8
- Total   23

Evil twins

Local legends tell of two different types of dragon in this part of Europe – the *zmaj* is **wise** and intelligent,

and not always hostile, while the *azdaja* is a **monster** of pure evil. Perhaps the modern dragon is a *zmaj*, and the dragon Jason fought was an *azdaja*?

47

CHINESE DRAGON

Fierce but wise, this Oriental **beast** looks very different from its European cousins, with a **snakelike** body, exquisite head, and **no wings**. Imbued with **magical powers**, they can fly, make themselves invisible – and even take on **human** form.

POWER: Wingless flight

Look – up in the sky! Is it a bird? No, it's a dragon! Even though they don't have **wings**, the Chinese variety can still fly, twisting through the air and turning graceful somersaults. According to tradition, they owe this **magical power** to lumps on their forehead known as a *chimu* or *chin-mu*.

TRACKING: Storm signs

A passing **storm** can indicate that Chinese **dragons** are dancing among the clouds using their wild, natural **magic**.

Water rulers

The Chinese say their dragons have power over weather and **water**. They often manifest themselves as waterspouts, and mighty **dragon kings** are said to rule over the **four seas** to the north, south, east, and west of China.

48

Nine into one

Chinese tales often describe dragons with features from nine separate animals – the head of a camel or horse with the horns of a stag, the ears of a cow and the eyes of a demon, the belly of a clam, the scales of a carp, the feet of a tiger with the claws of an eagle, and last but not least, the tail of a snake, often adorned with feathery plumes.

Most Chinese dragons have moustachelike tendrils sprouting from below their snouts. No one's ever got close enough to find out what they're for, but they're quite similar to the barbels on Chinese koi carp.

Dragon Battle

The air is torn by reptilian roars and buildings tumble as the Ljubljana dragon does midair battle with a Chinese dragon. People flee in panic, for the destruction can be terrible when mighty dragons clash . . . .

LAMBTON WORM

Slithering from the **depths** of the Earth comes this huge and **revolting** limbless dragon, known for **terrifying** the villagers of Fatfield in the north of England. **Crushing coils**, a vicious bite, the ability to heal itself instantly… would you be **brave enough** to **take it on?**

Hill chill

After ten years, the now **enormous** worm emerged from the well to **devour** sheep and villagers. It **killed** anyone who attacked it; if they managed to chop bits off, the **monster** just reattached them and healed instantly. It liked to **coil** itself around a local hill; you can still see the marks it left.

Hooked!

According to legend, a young man called John Lambton skipped church one Sunday to go fishing in the River Wear. He **snagged** a **slimy**, worm-like creature that **wriggled** and snapped at his hands … so he **threw** it down a well.

Well, well….

When John grew up, he went off to seek his fortune as a soldier. Meanwhile, in the well, the worm grew … and grew … AND **GREW**.

TACTIC: **Be sharp!**

John Lambton, now a famous knight, returned to **defeat** the worm. On advice of a local witch, he dressed in **spiked** and bladed armor.

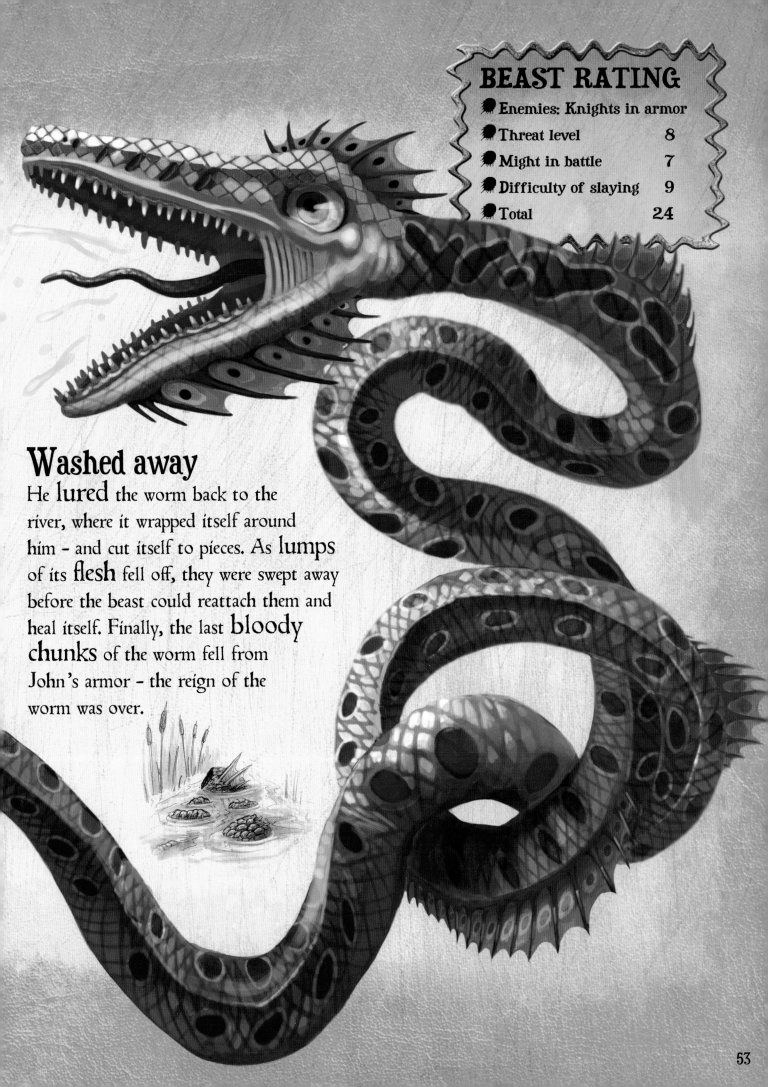

Washed away

He lured the worm back to the river, where it wrapped itself around him - and cut itself to pieces. As lumps of its flesh fell off, they were swept away before the beast could reattach them and heal itself. Finally, the last bloody chunks of the worm fell from John's armor - the reign of the worm was over.

JERSEY DEVIL

If you ever visit the forests of North America and hear **wild flapping** and unnerving screeching — beware! It may be the Jersey Devil, a hideous demonic dragon that has eluded capture for centuries. Small but horrifically vicious, it delights in terrifying travellers on **lonely** paths through the pines....

WANTED
ALIVE
~ THE ~
JERSEY
DEVIL
Reward: $10,000
Apply to: Philadelphia Zoo

Ancient weirdness

People first reported seeing the Jersey Devil in the New Jersey Pine Barrens in the early 1800s, but local Native Americans called the Barrens "the place of the dragon" long before European settlers turned up.

New monster in town

For decades, the few people who claimed to have seen the Jersey Devil were generally laughed at. Then, in January 1909, the devil sparked **terror** by appearing in several cities. In one place, it even gouged **chunks** out of a trolleybus!

WANTED!

The Philadelphia Zoo offered a $10,000 reward for the captured devil, but without success – hoaxers tried to sell them a kangaroo with fake wings on its shoulders! Meanwhile, the devil itself disappeared back home, where it still sometimes spooks travellers on the lonely roads of the Pine Barrens.

Devil child

One tale says that a local woman, called Mother Leeds, gave birth to twelve children – and swore that if she had another, it would be the devil. When her thirteenth child was born, it was a tiny monster with a demon's tail! It flew around the room before disappearing up the chimney!

TACTIC:
Follow the prints

Fresh snow preserved the Jersey Devil's cloven hoofprints, but hunting parties of police and soldiers searched in vain; often, just when they seemed to be getting close, the tracks came to an abrupt end where the devil had flown away.

BEAST RATING
- Enemies: Park rangers
- Threat level   6
- Might in battle   4
- Difficulty of slaying   6
- Total   16

WYVERN

Wyverns are one of the smaller types of **dragon**, but what they lack in size they make up for in **nastiness**. These two-legged terrors combine an **evil** temper with sharp **slashing** claws, a poisonous bite, and **fiery** breath. They're also fast and agile flyers, so keep an eye on the skies and be ready to **run** for cover!

WEAPON: Flying blowtorch

Specially adapted innards give the wyvern a **belch** to be reckoned with. They can blow out invisible (but stinky!) poisonous gas, or strike a **spark** on their flinty teeth to ignite their breath in a jet of deadly flames.

Armored hide

A wyvern's body is covered in **scales** that protect it from most threats – arrows, spears, and even **swords** will just bounce off, unless you can find one of the few **soft** parts on its skin....

Ancient heritage?

Some people think that wyverns could be descendants of pterodactyls - flying reptiles that ruled the skies millions of years ago, during the age of the dinosaurs.

Noble symbol

Wyverns are found mostly in western Europe, and particularly in mountainous areas. Back in the olden days, knights in armor would paint a wyvern on their shield to show they weren't to be messed with.

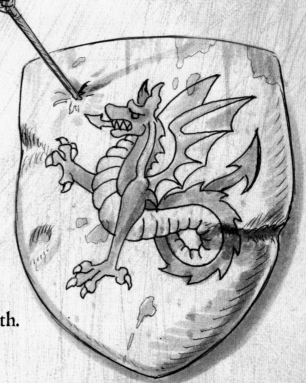

TIP: Watch the gargoyles!

These dragons are ambush hunters - and they like nothing better than perching on castle battlements (or the top of any old building) pretending to be a stone gargoyle. By the time you realize that the gargoyle is actually moving, it's usually too late!

BEAST RATING

- Enemies: Knights, soldiers
- Threat level   7
- Might in battle   8
- Difficulty of slaying   6
- Total   21

CHAPTER 4

Shapeshifters

With the power to shift from one **deadly** form to another, shapeshifters are the most **dangerously** deceptive **beasts** of all. Combining human intelligence and **cunning** with animal instinct and **strength**, they range from kidnappers and **tricksters** to brutal **predators**. If you hunt one down, be careful – you can never be **quite** sure what you're going to get!

Shapeshifters

2.5

2.0

1.5

1.0

0.5

0.0

WEREWOLF

- Howling at night
- Feasting on human flesh
- Freakish facial fur

SELKIE

- Murdering for revenge
- Generally acting very seal-like
- Being very drippy

Misdemeanors

KITSUNE

- Playing tricks on people in authority
- Using illusions that completely fox you
- Foxy behavior

SKINWALKER

- Preying on its own people
- Behaving like an animal
- Bear-faced lies

BANSHEE

- Screeching at night
- Being weird in the woods
- Foretelling death

WEREWOLF

Fur shimmering in the **moonlight**, the werewolf emerges from the woods, **blood** and drool dripping from its **slobbering** mouth. Lycanthropes have been feared for centuries; when the Full Moon is high in the sky, they go on the **prowl** and don't care whether it's **human** or animal **flesh** on the menu....

TACTIC: Look for bristles

There are various ways to spot a potential werewolf in between transformations. Eyebrows that meet in the middle and curly fingernails are signs – but plenty of normal people have both of those features, so check for bristles on the suspect's tongue to be sure.

Full Moon

Werewolves are only active for a few nights each month – around the Full Moon. Some say they must actually sleep in the moonlight to be transformed. A person may not realize they are a werewolf until they wake up with raw meat between their teeth....

TIP: Silver weapons

If you're looking to take down a werewolf, silver weapons are a must, be they bullets or an axe. But werewolves have far more strength than any human or wolf, so be very careful when you take your shot, and always have an escape route!

How-to guide

Some strange people deliberately transform themselves into werewolves. The right potion or ointment can summon this dark magic; sleeping in the Full Moon wearing a belt of wolfskin can also bring about the change.

BEAST RATING

- Enemies: Other shapeshifters, vampires
- Threat level   7
- Might in battle   7
- Difficulty of slaying   8
- Total   22

Dangerous bite

Whatever you do, don't let the werewolf sink his teeth into you – even if you manage to escape alive, it may pass the curse of lycanthropy on to you!

SELKIE

Ever get the feeling you're being **watched** when you walk along a deserted beach? Selkies and their kin are **untrustworthy** shapeshifters that rarely show their true form to humans, so watch out if you turn the next corner and find yourself face-to-face with a **beautiful lady** or man from the sea....

HABITAT: Orkney Islands

These beautiful and gentle seafolk are found across the North Atlantic Ocean, where they hide away in **seal** colonies. They're most commonly seen around the Orkney Islands of northern Scotland.

Watchers in the water

Selkies spend much of their lives in the form of seals, **watching** people from the safety of the sea. Because they are so **ungainly** on land, they have to shed their **magical skins** in order to shapeshift. On land, they take the form of handsome men or beautiful women who can make humans fall in love with them at first sight!

TACTIC: Hide the skin

Once on land, a selkie must hide and protect their enchanted sealskin, or they will never be able to return to the sea again. If you **need** to get the better of a selkie, find and **hide** its skin.

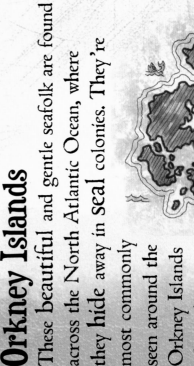

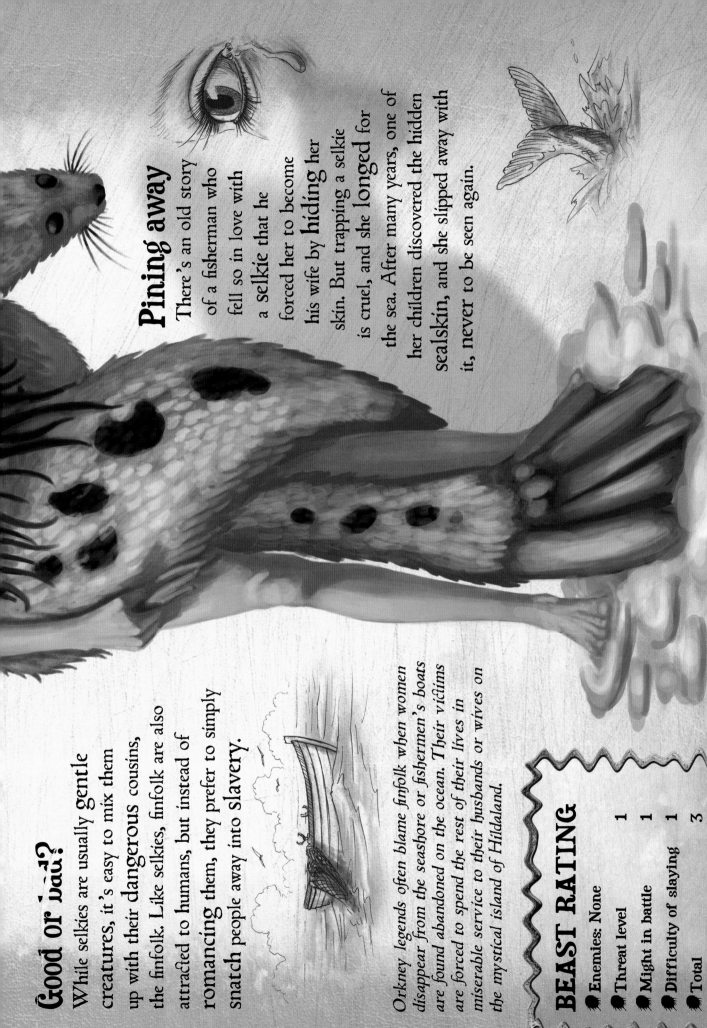

Pining away

There's an old story of a fisherman who fell so in love with a selkie that he forced her to become his wife by hiding her skin. But trapping a selkie is cruel, and she longed for the sea. After many years, one of her children discovered the hidden sealskin, and she slipped away with it, never to be seen again.

Good or bad?

While selkies are usually gentle creatures, it's easy to mix them up with their dangerous cousins, the finfolk. Like selkies, finfolk are also attracted to humans, but instead of romancing them, they prefer to simply snatch people away into slavery.

Orkney legends often blame finfolk when women disappear from the seashore or fishermen's boats are found abandoned on the ocean. Their victims are forced to spend the rest of their lives in miserable service to their husbands or wives on the mystical island of Hildaland.

BEAST RATING

- Enemies: None
- Threat level   1
- Might in battle   1
- Difficulty of slaying 1
- Total   3

KITSUNE

Silent and swift, elegant and cunning, the kitsune flit in the blink of an eye between the shape of a beautiful woman and their natural, foxy form. Some of these Japanese fox spirits are wise and kindly, many more revel in mischief-making, and some are just plain wicked. So be careful if you cross a kitsune's path, and watch out for the telltale tail!

WEAPONS: Lightning and lights

Kitsune can spit fire from their mouths or lightning from their tails, usually to defend themselves. But these natural tricksters also use their talents to create eerie lights called *kitsunebe* to lure unwary travellers off their paths.

Foxy faces

Kitsune can take a variety of human forms but most prefer the shape of young women. They often give themselves away through foxlike features, which Japanese people consider to be very beautiful. Alternatively, some kitsune can actually take possession of people to work their mischief in the human world.

Barking dog

Kitsune hate dogs, and dogs, as a rule, hate kitsune just as much. They also see straight through their disguises, so if your dog starts barking and snarling, don't be surprised to see that beautiful lady turn back into a fox and run for the hills!

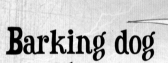

Tell-tails

Shapeshifted kitsune find it hard to keep their human form, and can give themselves away in several ways. Sometimes they cast a fox's shadow or reflection, and they have trouble hiding their tails, which can pop out at unexpected moments!

66

Nine-tailed wonders

Kitsune are very long-lived, and as they grow older and wiser, they gain more tails - first one, then five, then seven. The wisest and most powerful kitsune of all have nine tails, and are said to be able to see or hear everything in the world.

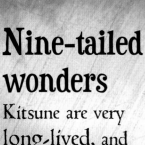

BEAST RATING

- Enemies: None
- Threat level — 3
- Might in battle — 3
- Difficulty of slaying — 2
- Total — 8

SKINWALKER

Driving through the Utah desert late at night, something **big** shambles across the road. Is it a bear? A big dog? It stops, stands straight up, and stares right at you ... then is gone, leaving you **frozen** in **terror**. You've just met a **skinwalker** – a cursed magician that Native Americans have learned to be **very scared of** ....

American outcasts

Many tribes tell tales of the skinwalkers. The Navajo's stories explain that skinwalkers started out as **shamans** (magicians) who broke the rules of **magic** in their thirst for power. Cast out from society, they now hide in the day and only emerge to **hunt** at night.

Skin-wearers

Skinwalkers have the **power** to transform into many different animals – wolves, foxes, bears, and even owls and crows. They **shift** their shape by wrapping themselves in the animal's pelt and using **forbidden** magical songs. **Transformations** can alter the whole body, or just certain parts.

Deadly stare

Wise Navajo agree that for all his strength, a skinwalker's **eyes** are his most **dangerous** weapon. Some say that if you make eye contact they can **paralyze** you and drain your life force. Others warn it's even worse – the skinwalker can take over your **body** and turn you into his puppet!

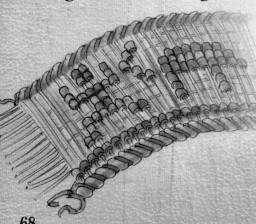

BEAST RATING

- **Enemies: All who threaten its people. werewolves**
- **Threat level**   5
- **Might in battle**   8
- **Difficulty of slaying**   9
- **Total**   22

A skinwalker takes on the abilities of the animal he has changed into – so he may be as fleet-footed as an antelope, as quiet as a fox, or as strong as a bear. Watch out when you're on the trail of one, because you never know what form he may take!

TIP:

White ash and name

The only way to kill a skinwalker face-to-face is to use **bullets** dipped in white ash from a fire. The Navajo say that if you can find out a skinwalker's **true name,** you can use it in a special **spell** that will rob them of their **powers.**

FOREST FIGHT

Deep in a wild North American forest, a pack of **werewolves** – called into their wild and ravenous state by the **eerie** lunar light – attack a bear-spirit **skinwalker**, but this monstrously powerful 'shifter swings a tree trunk and swats the **slobbering** beasts away as if they were flies....

BANSHEE

In the black of the **night**, an unearthly screech sends shivers down your spine. An owl? Maybe a fox? You'd better hope it wasn't the wail of the **banshee**, whose screams foretell **violent death**! Driven half-mad by their visions of the **bloody** future, they won't be reasoned with or silenced. Best you stick in your earplugs – and hide!

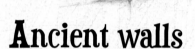

Ancient walls

Some haunt castles or stately homes, where their screams are said to foretell a **death** in the family. The banshee sometimes appears wandering along battlements, **tearing** at her clothes in grief.

TIP: Cover your ears!

The banshee's **cry** varies. In the west of Ireland it's said to be a low and **melodic** song, but in the east, it's a **piercing screech** loud enough to shatter glass. So if in doubt, cover your ears!

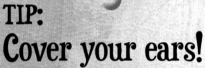

Animal forms

Like all **fairies**, banshees can shapeshift to take the form of animals – usually stoats, weasels, or hares. Their favorite form, however, is the **hooded crow**, which haunts wild woods and high mountains, and flocks to **battlefields** to feast on the flesh of the dead.

HABITAT: Ancient haunts

The word *banshee* means "woman of the burial mounds," and banshees are often found around ancient **grave mounds** in Britain and especially Ireland. Sometimes, you may stumble across them washing bloody **clothes** and **armor** in nearby rivers....

Banshees are the wildest of the fairy folk – although they can shapeshift to appear as beautiful girls with butterfly wings. When they let the illusion slip, they reveal their true form – tattered and ragged wings, worn and haggard features, and staring, hypnotic eyes.

BEAST RATING

- Enemies: None
- Threat level   4
- Might in battle   1
- Difficulty of slaying   9
- Total   14

CHAPTER 5

Trolls, Giants, AND Demons

Barren mountaintops and ancient woods are haunted by creatures far older than humanity – elemental beings from the First Age of the Earth. Some like nothing more than to meddle in the affairs of man, while others prefer to keep their distance in the remote wilderness. But all can be deadly when angered, and you cross them at your peril!

| 3.0 |
| 2.5 |
| 2.0 |
| 1.5 |
| 1.0 |
| 0.5 |
| 0.0 |

DRAUG

- Slaughtering mortals and stealing cattle
- Throwing curses
- Entering dreams without permission

BLACK SHUCK

- Making graveyards no-go areas
- Damaging church property
- Howling after 11 p.m.

JOTUN FROST GIANT

- Bringing winter five months early
- Freezing mortals to death
- Associating with renegade Norse gods

76

Crimes and Misdemeanors

Trolls, Giants, and Demons

KRAMPUS

- Kidnapping kids at Christmas
- Swapping presents for coal
- Terrifying children for fun

ELF

- Slaughtering trolls (even useful ones)
- Being madly mischievous
- Battling and brawling

TROLL

- Stealing and eating goats
- Fighting elves
- Being grumpy in charge of a bridge

DRAUG

Draugs are Viking **warriors** risen from the **dead**, anchored to the Earth by the fortune they pillaged in life. They cheated death to guard their riches, thus becoming stinking, demon **zombies**. They hate mortals and will kill any they see on their nightly roamings. Your only hope: track and **kill them first!**

Stinky strength

The draug may be little more than **rotting flesh** and bone, but he has the strength of ten fighting men. He can morph into a foul smoke, rising at will from his grave.

WEAPON: Magic axe

The draug's weapon, a special *skeggox*, or bearded axe, will cleave a mortal in two. Charms, written in **runic** script, bestow **magical** properties in combat, the axe seeking and targeting an opponent's weakest point.

TIPS: Scissors and spells

Iron scissors left open on the corpse's chest will cut the soul and stop them becoming a draug; and to stop a draug haunting your nightmares, carve a spell on a stone and hurl it on the grave.

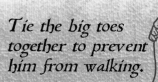

Tie the big toes together to prevent him from walking.

Rode rage

There is no sight more terrifying than a draug on the rampage. They steal bulls for the thrill of it, riding the snorting creatures into **demented** frenzy. Some say it is the draug's smell that torments the bulls; others the pain of the rattling **bones** on their back. The bulls are **dead** by dawn.

Dried twigs hidden in the clothes may suck up evil desires.

TRACKING: Follow the stench!

The demon draug leaves no tracks where he passes. But you can **smell** him a mile distant. When the air is thick with an **evil stench**, you know a draug is close. Follow his foul scent to **hunt** him down.

TO VANQUISH:
Attack and behead it

Leap at it with a longsword and **sever its head**. Bury it at a crossroads and burn the **body** on a pyre. Only then is the draug truly **dead**.

BEAST RATING

- Enemies: Mortals
- Threat level — 8
- Might in battle — 8
- Difficulty of slaying — 7
- Total — 23

BLACK SHUCK

What's that in the darkness? A whisper-quiet padding of huge paws, an unearthly howl, the glow of flaming eyes - and the demon-dog black shuck is on you in an instant!. Whether it's a warner of imminent death, or just a watcher over souls in graveyards, this dog's bite is worse than its bark!

WEAPON: Burning claws

The shuck's claws are vicious. Some believe they can be scorchingly hot!

HABITAT: Graves and lanes

Black shucks have terrified village dwellers in Northern Europe for centuries. They prowl around dark lanes and graveyards, lurking amongst the shadows and misty hollows....

WARNING: Storm signs

Their appearance is often foreshadowed by sudden storms - with lightning strikes. (The shuck can cause as much destruction as lightning itself. In 1577, one destroyed a church steeple.)

A shuck's hideous howl will make your blood run cold. If you hear one, you'd best shut your eyes; seeing a shuck may mean you will meet a hideous fate!

The burnt slashes on this church door (in a village called Bungay) were made by a black shuck's hot claws; locals call the burns "the devil's scorch marks."

BEAST RATING

- Enemies: Mortals
- Threat level   6
- Might in battle   8
- Difficulty of slaying   9
- Total   23

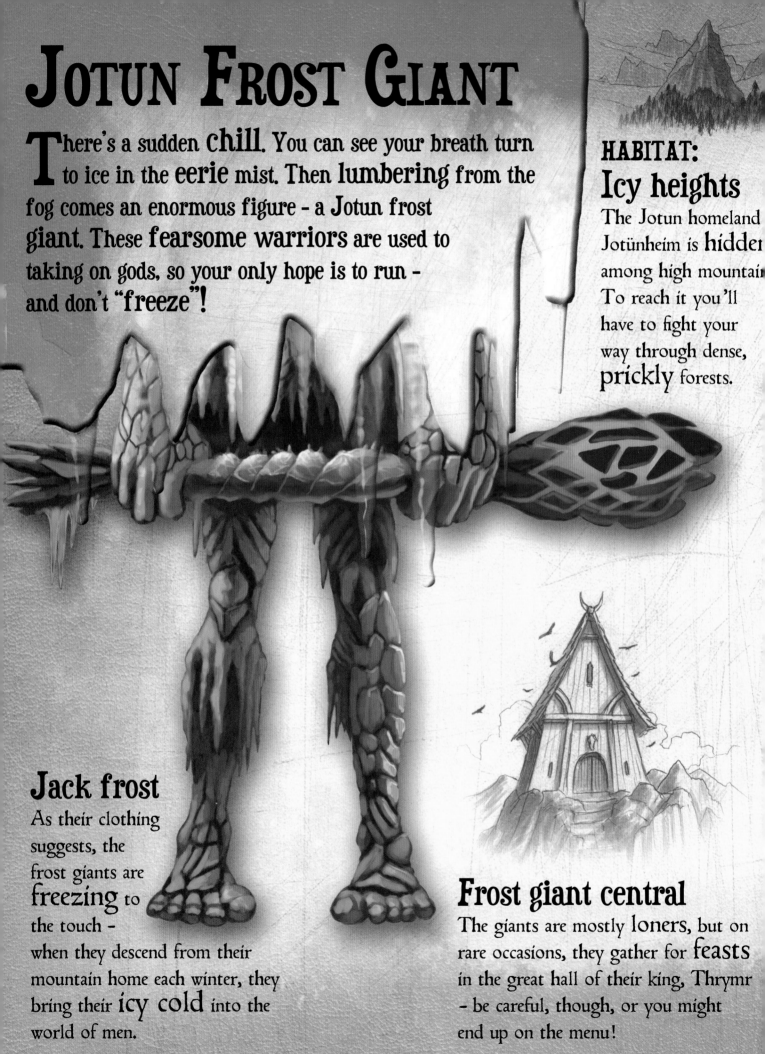

JOTUN FROST GIANT

There's a sudden **chill**. You can see your breath turn to ice in the **eerie** mist. Then **lumbering** from the fog comes an enormous figure - a Jotun frost giant. These **fearsome warriors** are used to taking on gods, so your only hope is to run - and don't "**freeze**"!

HABITAT: Icy heights

The Jotun homeland Jotünheim is **hidden** among high mountain. To reach it you'll have to fight your way through dense, **prickly** forests.

Jack frost

As their clothing suggests, the frost giants are **freezing** to the touch - when they descend from their mountain home each winter, they bring their **icy cold** into the world of men.

Frost giant central

The giants are mostly **loners**, but on rare occasions, they gather for **feasts** in the great hall of their king, Thrymr - be careful, though, or you might end up on the menu!

WEAPON:
Mighty club

Frost **giants** use huge clubs to fight Norse gods such as Thor – or to flatten **puny** mortals!

Figure in the fog

They are often glimpsed as vast, **sinister shapes** in distant mountain mists and **impenetrable fog.**

Viking soothsayers tell that one day the Jotun will descend from their mountain lairs, spreading icy winter across the world. The great ash tree Yggdrasil, which supports the world, will shake, heralding Ragnarok, the devastating final battle between the Jotun and the Norse gods.

BEAST RATING

- Enemies: Norse gods, mortals
- Threat level 8
- Might in battle 9
- Difficulty of slaying 9
- Total 26

KRAMPUS

Ho ho ... NO! The Krampus is on his way, wishing you a not-so-happy holiday! This demon from the highest Alpine mountains is Santa's evil twin. It punishes naughty children and terrifies good ones! If you hear his chains on **Christmas Eve**, bury your head in the pillow – and don't peek out!

Naughty or nice?

The Krampus turns up at the same time as Santa – but while good kids get presents from Santa's bag of goodies, bad children get stuffed into the Krampus's sack and carried away to his lair.

WARNING: Rattling racket

While Santa's arrival is announced by gentle sleigh bells, the Krampus wraps himself in **chains** and rusty cowbells to scare children. Cover your ears to protect yourself!

WEAPON: Whip or twigs

The Krampus carries a bundle of birch twigs, which he uses to beat naughty children. Sometimes he even leaves the bundle behind, pinned to a wall as a reminder to be good next year!

TRACKING:
Cloven prints

The Krampus's hairy legs and cloven hooves show his beastly nature – you may be able to track him from his goatlike footprints in the snow, but make sure he doesn't spot you as he'll easily run you down.

Black Christmas

Children who aren't bad enough to be beaten or dragged off in the Krampus's sack, but aren't good enough to get presents, wake up to find their Christmas stockings have been stuffed – with coal!

BEAST RATING

- Enemies: Naughty children
- Threat level   5
- Might in battle   4
- Difficulty of slaying 6
- Total   15

ELF

Most elves are mean-spirited, mischievous, and downright dangerous. Armed to the teeth, athletic, and fast-moving, they have keen eyesight and hearing and will spot you long before you see them. Our advice? Be polite, watch out for tricks, and if all else fails, carry something shiny and expensive - elves love treasure!

Shapeshifters

There are many different types of elf and related creatures - some looking beautiful and some demonic. But whatever their appearance, all elves are troublesome, unpredictable, and violent creatures underneath.

TRACKING: Fairy rings

Elves love a raucous party, chasing each other in circles at dawn and dusk, and leaving these distinctive rings of mushrooms to mark the trails of their dancing. Don't be misled by the term "fairy ring" - there's nothing fairylike about them!

TACTIC: Make your mark

When they're not fighting, elves love to play tricks - bu they can only enter your hous if they're invited. Drawing th elf cross on your front door warns them that they're n welcome and protects yo from their mischief.

BEAST RATING

- Enemies: Mortals, trolls
- Threat level — 7
- Might in battle — 6
- Difficulty of slaying — 7
- Total — 20

One favorite trick of the elves is to kidnap human babies from their cradles, switching them for their own elvish young.

WEAPON: Knives

Elves are ferocious fighters, always spoiling for a battle and armed to the hilt. Equipped with the vicious blades, they'll slice and dice anyone they don't like the look of – whether that's a human, a troll, or another elf.

War of the Elves

As the elf clans **swarm** onto the plain, the **battle** reaches fever pitch, **corpses** mingling with the churned mud below. As sabres clash, a **filthy troll** rises up from his underground lair, **spitting** elf **blood and guts**....

TROLL

Nasty, brutish, tall, and ugly, trolls are **enormous**, **ferocious**, and always hungry! If you're venturing into troll territory, you'd better take a goat in case one catches your scent. The best time to go troll hunting is just before dawn – they're **creatures** of the night, and tend to "go to pieces" in **daylight!**

Favorite snack

Trolls are famously greedy – they'll eat anything, but **goat meat** is their favorite food of all. Leave an unguarded goat tethered in troll territory, and there won't be much left the following day!

Deadly sniffers

These beefy giants may be famously slow-witted, but they have an incredible **sense of smell**, and can sniff out humans over several miles. The smell of Christians, who drove them away from their traditional lands, makes them particularly **mad**.

Deadly sunrise

Most trolls are **night hunters**, retreating to caves or under their bridges during the day. For some species, this is just because they prefer the night, but if certain types of troll are caught in **direct sunlight**, a chemical reaction **can turn them to stone.**

TACTIC: Ring out!

Trolls don't like **loud noises**, and in particular they hate the sound of church bells. Take a small bell with you for protection on any **troll-hunting** expeditions.

HABITAT: Bridges and hollows

Trolls like to make their homes **under bridges,** which provide shade in the daytime, a ready supply of water, and a good place to lie in wait for **unwary travellers.**

BEAST RATING

- Enemies: Mortals, elves
- Threat level   8
- Might in battle   9
- Difficulty of slaying   7
- Total   24

GLOSSARY

ATHENIANS – people of Athens, Greece.

AZDAJA – a vile, cruel East European dragon of pure evil.

AZTECS – the people of old Central Mexico, from between the fourteenth and seventeenth centuries. They created a powerful, colorful civilization, and built great cities with astonishing temples and pyramids.

BANSHEE – a type of terrifying female spirit from Ireland, famed for its blood-chilling wail.

BLACK SHUCK – an English demon-dog.

BOKOR – a voodoo priest.

CADAVER – a dead body.

CENTAURS – half-human, half-horse warriors from ancient Greek myth.

CHIMU, OR CHIN-MU – the magical bumps on a Chinese dragon's head that give these wingless wonders the power of flight.

CLOVEN HOOF – a hoof divided down the middle into two parts, such as that of a goat ... or a devil.

CRETE – a Greek island in the eastern Mediterranean Sea, site of the Minoan civilization.

CYCLOPS – a massive one-eyed giant from ancient Greek myths.

DEVIL – a beast of pure evil, usually with horns, a tail, and cloven hooves.

DEITY – a god.

DRAGON – a monstrous reptile, usually capable of flying and breathing fire, sometimes with four legs, sometimes with none, but always fierce.

DRAUG – an undead Viking warrior.

ELF – a small, skilled, and vicious race of supernatural beast, often mistakenly thought to be nice.

GARGOYLE – a hideous and fantastic dragonlike monster, shown in stone on many old churches and other buildings.

GORGON – one of three sisters – Stheno, Euryale, and Medusa – from ancient Greek myth, with snakes for hair and the power to turn men to stone with a glance.

GREEK HEROES – the strong, brave, and clever warriors of ancient Greek myths, who managed to defeat many a monster, using cunning and help from their gods.

HABITAT – the place a beast likes to dwell.

HINDU – belonging to Hinduism, a religion from India, full of extraodinary stories and deities.

IMPALE – to stick a stake or other large sharp object through something – or some beast.

JIANG SHI – a Chinese hopping zombie.

JOTUN FROST GIANT – gigantic icy megamonsters of Norse myth.

KITSUNE – magical Japanese foxes capable of taking human form.

KRAMPUS – a devilish beast that appears in countries around the Alps, infamous for punishing and scaring children in the festive season.

LABYRINTH – the complicated maze built for King Minos as a place to keep the Minotaur.

LYCANTHROPE – the scientific name for a werewolf; lycanthropy is the power to turn into a wolf.

MINOAN – belonging to this ancient civilization from Crete, ruled by King Minos.

MINOTAUR – the part-bull, part-man beast that dwelled in the labyrinth.

MISDEMEANORS – acts of appalling behavior or mischief.

MORTALS – normal human beings – such as you …?

MYTH – an ancient story so mysterious that no one knows what part of it is made up and what is true.

NAGA – a spirit or beast from Hindu and Buddhist myth, often female, that combines human features with those of a serpent.

NAVAJO – a Native American Indian people, from the lands we now call New Mexico and Arizona.

NORSE – of ancient Scandinavia, especially the Vikings. Norse myths are full of huge strong heroes, enormous ultrapowerful beasts, and mighty deities.

PETRIFYING – usually used to mean "very frightening," this word actually means something that is turning – or can turn you – into stone.

PHYSICIAN – a doctor.

REPELLENTS – substances that drive a being away, such as garlic to a vampire.

SELKIE – sea beast from waters of the coastal islands around Scotland. Selkies live as seals in the sea but transform into women when on land.

SERPENT – a snake or similar reptile, usually evil.

SHAPESHIFTER – a human with the ability to become an animal.

SKINWALKER – in Native American Indian myth, a person with the power to transform into any animal he or she desires.

SLOVENIA – a Central European state. Its capital city is Ljubljana.

SUPERNATURAL – something that is "above nature" and beyond normal explanation, such as a magical power or being.

TACTIC – a way to approach a problem or difficult task … such as defeating a beast.

TROLL – a large, grumpy, lumpy, ugly beast, usually dwelling in a cave or under a bridge.

UNDEAD – a being that once died but now lives again in a horrid, deathlike state.

VAMPIRE – a being that feeds on living creatures, usually by drinking their blood.

VENOM - a naturally made poison, usually squirted at or injected into its victims.

VIKINGS - the fierce pirate traders and raiders from Scandinavia who caused havoc on the coasts of Northern Europe between the eighth and eleventh centuries.

WEREWOLF - a human partly or totally transformed into a wolf.

WYVERN - a smaller species of dragon, possibly venomous, sometimes fire-breathing, often shown on shields.

XOLOTL - the dog-headed Aztec god of lightning and death who protects the Sun.

YGGDRASIL - in Norse myth, the great tree of life that supports this and all other worlds.

ZMAJ - a wise Eastern European dragon, fierce but fair.